The Friendly Witch

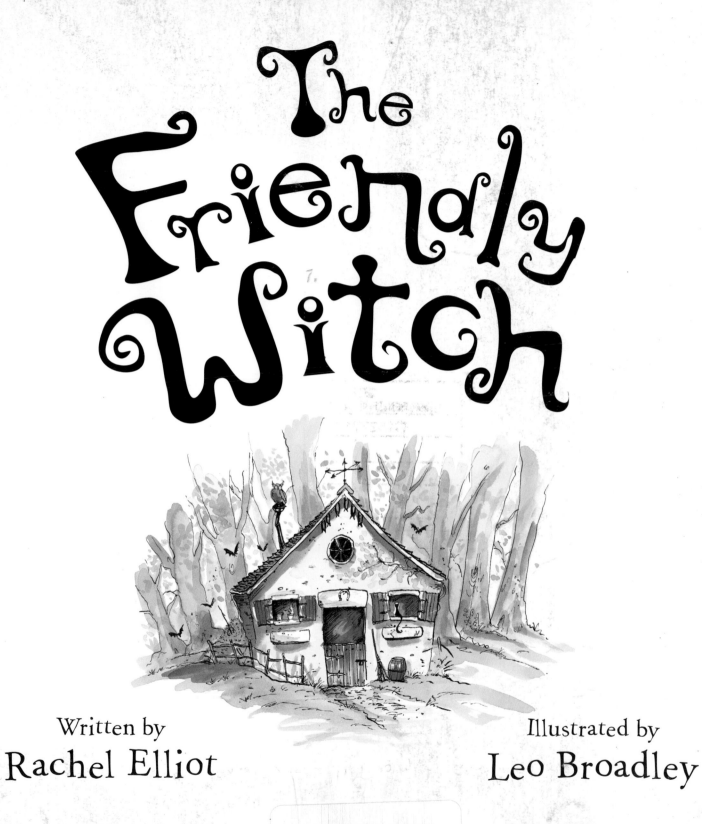

Written by
Rachel Elliot

Illustrated by
Leo Broadley

It was very quiet in the forest.

Today was the Friendly Witch's birthday
(she wouldn't say how old she was).

But she didn't have any cards.

She didn't have any presents.
She didn't have any visitors.

"And that is the last straw!"
said the Friendly Witch.

"I wish I could have a little birthday party!" she said sadly.

But as you know, witches don't have fairy godmothers to grant them wishes. So she decided to make a spell herself...

...a special spell for visitors.

"I hope I can remember how,"
thought the Friendly Witch.
It was a long time since she had made
a spell (and that had only been a
basic prince-into-a-frog potion).

She mixed all the ingredients up
in her cauldron and whispered, what
she hoped, were the secret magic words.

Suddenly there was a loud knock
on the door.

"It's worked!" said the Friendly Witch...

"I don't have much room!"
exclaimed the Friendly Witch.

"But you're all very welcome!"

Goldilocks was first through
the door (with all three bears).
"Any porridge?"
asked Baby Bear hopefully.
Beauty and the Beast came in
holding hands!
"Try to remember your table
manners," she whispered to him.

Goosey Goosey Gander
waddled in, holding a left shoe.
"It's wasn't me!" he said.
"He just fell!"

"I wouldn't believe him if I
were you," said Little Bo Peep.
"You haven't seen my sheep,
by any chance?

Mary Mary turned her nose
up at the garden.
"No silver bells or cockle shells,"
she said. "What a disgrace."

"I like my little nut trees,"
said the Friendly Witch,
feeling a bit upset.
"The King of Spain's daughter
came to see them once,
you know."

Humpty Dumpty was telling the
third little pig all about his latest fall.
"I'm accident-prone," he boasted.

"All the king's horses and
all the king's men are outside,
just in case!".

"She should have built this cottage
out of brick," said the third little pig,
who wasn't listening.

"I could teach her a thing
or two!".

Miss Muffet was looking for some curds and whey when a spider turned up.

"Help! Help! A horrible spider!" she screamed. "Why do they need that many legs?"

"I love spiders," cried the Friendly Witch. "They catch the flies!"
"I swallowed a fly once," said an old woman in her ear. "Long story."

"Could I have a bone for my dog?"
asked Mother Hubbard.
"Sorry, but my cupboards are bare!"
said the Friendly Witch.

The Fairy Godmother appeared
in a puff of sparkling smoke.
"I can't stay long!" she snapped.
"I have to stop Sleeping Beauty
snoring before the prince gets there."

"Does anybody want to see a
magic trick?" called Aladdin,
clutching an old lamp.
"I've seen it all before,"
said the Fairy Godmother.

"Don't rub that lamp!"
shouted the Friendly Witch.
"There's no room for a...

CRRRACK!

"Too late!" exclaimed Aladdin.

"Who invited the genie?" grumbled Rumpelstiltskin, who could hardly squeeze into the packed little cottage. "He's standing on my beard!"

Just when the Friendly Witch
thought it couldn't get any
louder, a fine lady rode up
on a white horse.
"I must have music
wherever I go,"
said the fine
lady, haughtily.
She had rings on her
fingers and bells on
her toes. She was followed by
the Pied Piper (and far too many rats for comfort).

Old King Cole's fiddlers three struck up a catchy tune.
The Sugar Plum Fairy was teaching the big bad wolf how to pirouette (he really wanted to dance with one of the three little pigs). The twelve dancing princesses waltzed in, looking for partners.

"There isn't really room for that!" cried the Friendly Witch.

"Not more princesses," sighed the Fairy Godmother.
Simple Simon asked Red Riding Hood to dance but she stuck her tongue out at him (she wasn't a very polite little girl).

"I wish they would all leave me alone!"

The peace!
The silence!

It was wonderful to have
the cottage to herself again!

It was very quiet in the forest.

The Friendly Witch didn't
have any music.

She didn't have any dancing.
She didn't even have any visitors.

And after a while she started to wonder
if the party had really been all that bad.
"After all, it would be nice to have a few
visitors again," she sighed.

"Sometimes I wish..."

For Anne and Bill,
with love.

R.E.

Michelle, my wife
and soul mate.

L.B.

First published in 2005
by Meadowside Children's Books
185 Fleet Street, London, EC4A 2HS

Text © Rachel Elliot 2005
Illustrations © Leo Broadley 2005

The rights of Rachel Elliot
and Leo Broadley to be identified as the author
and illustrator of this work have been asserted
by them in accordance with the Copyright,
Designs and Patents Act, 1988

A CIP catalogue record for this book
is available from the British Library

Printed in China

10 9 8 7 6 5 4 3 2 1